My life

PUP

With thanks to Heather Ridley and her puppy Moonseal Pasadena (Thumbelina): all the websites for use of their images and information on pages 60-64: and to the 'A Kid's Guide to the Movies' by Jonathan Clements for movie information.

First published in Great Britain in 2003
The Chicken House
2 Palmer Street
Frome
Somerset
BA11 1DS

Produced and edited by Penny Worms
Designed by Robert Walster

Printed and bound in Great Britain

British Library Cataloguing in Publication data available

ISBN 1 904442 04 8

My life as a PUP

Words by Sarah Delmege

Illustrations by Richard Morgan
Photography by Tracy Morgan

The Chicken House

To all the Poppys of the world.
And all the Charlies too.
xxx

Chapter One

Hi! Hi there! Hi! Hi! I'm Poppy.
I'm a puppy. Do you like me? I like you.
Sniff. Sniff.

Hello! You smell good. Sniff. Sniff! Mmmm. You smell friendly. And clean. All soapy and shampooey! Yum, yum, double scrum.

Lemon shampoo. That's my favourite. That's what Molly smells of. She's my owner.

I love her. **LOADS**. Even more than choc drops. AND chopped liver! She's super-great.

THUMP. THUMP.

She loves me too. She ruffles my fur and pats me. **Pat. Pat. Pat. Pant. Pant.** Wag. Wag.

AND when she's eating dinner she sneaks me bits off her plate when she thinks no one is looking. Wag! Wag! She gets in **BIG** trouble when her dad catches her.
But she still does it.

Oh wow! She is great!

She makes me happy. Roll on the floor, paws in the air, bottom shuffle happy.

And, **WOW**, am I lucky! Molly adopted me when I was a really little, tiny tiny puppy. She says I was a cute bundle of fur with big brown eyes. She took one look and fell totally in love. And it was the same for me.
Wag. Wag.

What happened before then makes me SAD. But I'll tell you because you are my friend . . .

The lady who took me away from my mummy, brothers and sisters was horrible to me. She hurt me and then she left me, tied me to a lamp post. All alone. I was SCARED and **FRIGHTENED**. But then a nice man found

me. **Wag. Wag.** He took me to the London Dogs' Home.

At first I didn't like it there. It was big and noisy and SCARY. Someone took my photo and put me in a cage with this label on the front...

POPPY

Breed: Havanese

Age when arrived: Four weeks

Place found/recovered: Tied to a lamp post outside Clapham Junction train station.

Condition when found: Very hungry. Hadn't been fed for two or three days. Covered in bruises and jumping with fleas. Otherwise well.

Temperament: Very excitable and extremely friendly. No problem to handle.

Special Notes: Good with children. Will have no problem being re-housed.

But then I met **BERNIE**...

BERNIE

Breed: Bull Mastiff

Age when arrived: 8 years

Place found/recovered: Elderly owner died.

Condition when found: Extremely healthy. Obviously well loved and looked after.

Temperament: can be very sad and often mopes around. Probably missing owner.

Special Notes: Bernie is an extremely large dog. This means there could be a problem re-housing him.

Bernie was in the cage next to me. Now he's my best dog friend. I **LOVE** him. Even more than doggie chews. **Woof. Woof.**

He looked after me while I was there. He's wise and good. I didn't want to leave him. Molly could see how I felt and she wanted to take **Bernie** home with us too. But Molly's mum and dad said he was so big there just wasn't enough room for him in their house. Now they send him special doggie treats every month so he knows we haven't forgotten him. Molly's mum and dad are ***SUPER-GREAT!***

Bernie taught me loads and loads of things. He taught me the *Rules of Doghood*. Very important.

The most important things EVER.

Wowzer!

At eight weeks every single dog in the world becomes an ...um ...er ...what was the word now?...oh yes ...an **initiated** member of dogkind. (Wow oh wow, what a big word!)

Boy oh boy. It's very **VERY** important to stick to these rules. Otherwise every single dog in the whole wide world could suffer.

There are a lot of things to remember.

Wow oh wow. It took **Bernie** AGES to teach them all to me.

Once you've learnt all the rules by heart, you get a certificate. You have to put your paw print at the bottom to say you've agreed to all the rules and then bury the certificate some-where safe.

Mine is buried under the third tree on the right in the garden at the London Dogs' Home. **Wag. Wag.**

Because you are my friend I am going to share the rules with you. But you must never **EVER** tell anyone ...

To be obeyed at all times.
The Rules must never fall into the hands of humans.

I, POPPY, WILL NEVER EVER LET ON THAT DOGS CAN SPEAK AND UNDERSTAND HUMAN FLUENTLY. ANY SUCH ERROR COULD RESULT IN HUMANS DISCOVERING THAT DOGS ARE REALLY MUCH MORE INTELLIGENT THAN THEY GIVE US CREDIT FOR AND OUR LIVES OF LUXURY AND RELAXATION COULD BE OVER.

I agree to:

1. Only communicate in woofs, pants, whines and growls whenever any other human is within earshot.
2. Pretend to hate cats.
3. Chase and return sticks or any such object that a human chooses to throw, no matter how childish/puppyish, irritating or pointless the game may seem.
4. Pretend any tricks my owner teaches me are really hard, even though I could really do them blindfold, paws tied behind my back and standing on my head.
5. Show my owner huge amounts of affection AT ALL TIMES.

I have read and agree to abide by all the above rules.

Signed:

Poppy

I don't know where I'd have been without **Bernie**. He is very clever - not as clever as Alfie though. Alfie is probably the smartest dog in the world. Sometimes when we were in the Home he used such long words it made my head hurt just listening to him! **Wowzer!**

ALFIE

Breed: *Afghan hound*

Age when arrived: *Four years*

Place found/recovered: *The reading room of Stoke Newington Library.*

Condition when found: *Cold and hungry - he was surrounded by pages torn from books, obviously to keep himself warm.*

Temperament: *Very calm, but irritable around children and cats.*

Special Notes: *Alfie is quiet and docile. Would suit elderly owner.*

ALFIE was adopted by Professor Pemberton. They are perfect partners as the Professor has **loads** of books. Alfie buries his head in them whenever the Professor goes out. Boy, does Alfie love books. Almost as much as I love Molly. And that's **LOADS**. He is one clever dog.

And then there was **MAVIS**. She made me laugh.

MAVIS

Breed: *Irish water spaniel*
Age when arrived: *Ten years*
Place found/recovered: *Walthamstow Market - next to a fruit and veg stall.*
Condition when found: *Extremely well fed and groomed.*
Temperament: *Very intuitive and well behaved.*
Special Notes: *Mavis isn't keen on being walked. Seems to understand everything you say!*

MAVIS is a real Cockney from the East End of London. She was adopted by Stella, a fortune teller. And now they travel round the world with a fair. How exciting is that?

Woof. Woof.

And the last dog in our little pack was Tallulah. She lives in Los Angeles in America now, with a real-life celebrity. Oh boy, oh boy. Is she **LUCKY!**

TALLULAH

Breed: Miniature poodle

Age when arrived: Fifteen months

Place found/recovered: Sitting outside Harrod's in Knightsbridge.

Condition when found: Extremely well groomed.

Temperament: Can be stand-offish. Not very affectionate or friendly.

Special Notes: Tallulah refuses point-blank to walk on any concrete surface and has to be carried on all such occasions.

But don't get me wrong, I'm not in the least bit jealous of Tallulah!

I'm really lucky myself. **Wag. Wag.**

I now live in Molly's lovely house with her and her mum and dad and her little brother. He is called Nathan. I LOVE him. He throws sticks for me. **Wag. Wag.** And helps me dig for bones and hidden treasure in the garden. Molly's dad tells him off for this. A lot. But we still do it. **Wag. Wag.**

I **LOVE** my house. It's great. There's so much to do! **Wag. Wag.** There's a big fire to doze in front of in the lounge. A **huge** garden with loads of flowers to dig up. And I get to bark whenever people walk past.

Woof. Woof.

Plus there's Charlie. He's Molly's cat. We're great mates. But we pretend not to like each other when Molly, her mum and dad or Nathan are around. Oh boy, is Charlie funny.

Oh yeah, Baby! I'm as sharp as my claws! Signed Charlie XX

Charlie uses me as a pillow and sleeps on me. A lot. I like that.

10 Other Things That Make Me Happy

1. My dog bowl. It's shiny. I can carry it in my mouth. And it has **POPPY** spelt in big letters round the side. **Wag. Wag.** When it's empty, I am sad.

2. Food stealing. This happens when anyone leaves any food out. I get told off a lot for this. **Sigh!**

3. Breakfast. Yum, yum, bum scrum.

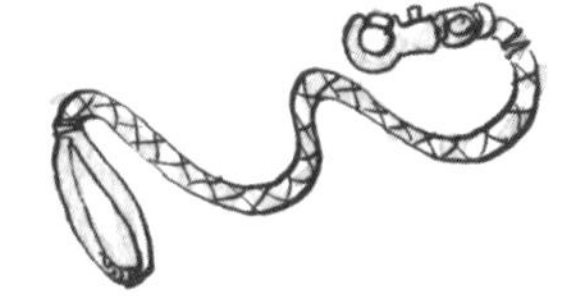

4. WALKIES. I love walkies. At least twice a day. **Wag. Wag.**

5. Playing ball. Chase, chase.
Pant. Pant.

6. Lunch. **Wag. Wag.**
Thump. Thump!

7. Playing 'Fetch'. But sometimes I am naughty and play 'Don't Fetch'. This makes Molly cross. **Woof. Woof.**

8. Having baths. **Mmmm.** Water! splash, splash! I love shaking my fur dry. This makes Molly scream and giggle.
Wag. Wag.

9. Swimming. I love water. I'm very good. Even better than Nathan who has to wear arm bands.

10. Supper. Mmmmm.
Food. Need I say more.
Thump. Thump!

Chapter Two

Yeah. Amazingly stupid!!! Charlie XXX

I am curled up on the sofa with Molly.
Her mum is upstairs vacuuming.
Molly is watching TV.

I am VERY comfy. **Mmmmm.** I might sleep now. **Wag. Wag.** Molly ruffles my head. AND strokes my ears. Paws up. Tummy rub.

Wow oh wow.

I love Molly.

GREAT HUGE ENORMOUS

amounts. More than any food. Ever. Even more than gravy. And boy, do I love gravy.

YUM!

Charlie jumps on the sofa and sits on my head. I growl. FIERCELY. He winks at me, then hisses, jumps off and strolls over to the fire. He is funny. Hee hee.

But I am wide awake now. I open one eye and watch TV with Molly.

Wow oh wow oh wow. Am I glad I am not asleep! The MOST INTERESTING TV show is on. In The Whole Wide World. Ever.

That's a matter of opinion, Charlie XX

Boy oh boy. It's all about the most amazing creatures in the world. Dogs! **Woof. Woof. Aroof!**

Oh my. Oh my. This HAS got to be the MOSTEST BESTEST thing EVER. Even better than peanut butter. **Wag. Wag**. There's so much stuff I didn't know. And, till now, I didn't even know I didn't know it! Wow oh wow!

There are so many interesting, dog-tastic facts, it's made my head hurt! Here's what the programme had to say ...

DOGTASTIC FACTS

Hey kids... And welcome to another episode of Animal World. This week, it's a dog's life. Yep, that's right, today we'll be giving you the low-down on 'man's best friend.' So if you're sitting comfortably and not feeling too ruff (ha ha!) we'll begin...

FACT 1

Here's your first fascinating fact. Did you know, most pet dogs are able to run at speeds of up to 30 km/h? And that the greyhound, the king of canine speedsters, is capable of reaching speeds of up to 64 km/h?

Bet you didn't know that pet cats can run as fast as 48 km/h. No wonder you can never catch me, you old slowcoach!
Love Charlie XX

FACT 2

And do you know why a frightened dog puts its tail between its legs? So that its scent glands are covered. The tail-between-the-legs behaviour is the doggie equivalent of me or you hiding our faces whenever we feel scared.

Yeah, either that or because you're butt-ugly!
Charlie XX

FACT 3

And here's another mind-blowing fact for you... The notion that cats and dogs are natural enemies is overstated if not totally false. Generally speaking, cats and dogs get along better than cats and cats or dogs and dogs.

That's a matter of opinion! Tee hee!
Charlie XX

FACT 4

If you're wondering what breeds of dog are the smartest, wonder no more. We've got the answer for you. In order, the cleverest dogs are:

1) border collie
2) poodle
3) golden retriever

I notice you're not there, Poppy! Why doesn't that surprise me?
Charlie XX

FACT 5

And the dumbest dog in the world is the Afghan hound. Yep, kids, the good old Afghan is definitely not the sharpest knife in the drawer.

He obviously hasn't met Alfie, eh Poppy?
Charlie XX

FACT 6

If you're going on a dog-spotting holiday, then make sure you head for the United States and France. Almost one in three families there own a dog. But if you're allergic then pack yourself off to Germany or Switzerland, as they only have one dog for every ten families.

Enough about dogs already. What about cats? Charlie XX

FACT 7

And that's not the only thing that dogs are better at than us humans. They can hear high-pitched sounds (such as the noise some insects make) that we can't even detect.

PARDON?
Oh, the old ones are the best ones. HEE HEE
Charlie XX

FACT 8

If you come across a German shepherd, look out. This breed of dog actually bites humans more than any other kind. That's one dog whose bark certainly isn't worse than his bite! Ha! Ha!

FACT 9

Talking of strange, did you know that Newfoundland dogs have webbed feet, making them strong and agile swimmers? And next time you're moaning that you have to take your dog out for a walk, spare a thought for ancient Chinese royalty. They used to carry Pekingese dogs in the sleeves of their royal robes.

That's obviously who Tallulah thinks she's descended from then.
Charlie XX

FACT 10

And I bet you didn't know that there are 701 types of purebred dog.

FACT 11

Talking of clothes, did you know that six out of ten dogs own a sweater, winter coat or raincoat? And that most owners have bought their dog some kind of jewellery? There are certainly some fashionable dogs out there!

FACT 12

And how's this for a weird fact? The bloodhound is the only animal in the world whose evidence can be used in an American court.

FACT 13

And if you're a dog owner, make sure you empty your bin regularly. A dog's sense of smell is a whopping 1,000 times better than a human's.

FACT 14

And, finally, here are a couple of dogs who would need their outfits tailor-made. The world's heaviest and longest dog ever recorded was an Old English mastiff named Zobra. He weighed a whopping 156kg. That's as much as two grown men! And the smallest dog was a tiny Yorkie from Blackburn, England. At two years of age and fully grown this little dog weighed only 113g and was the size of a matchbox. Bless. I don't know about you, but I'd be scared about treading on him!

Anyway kids, that's it for this show. I hope you've enjoyed learning all about dogs and that you'll join us at the same time next week when we'll be entering the weird and wonderful world of elephants. See you then!

Oh dear, oh dear, I didn't like the glint in Molly's eye when the presenter said that most owners admit that their dog owns a sweater or a coat.

Oh my, I have a bad feeling. Last time Molly looked like that she put lots and lots of make-up on Nathan, put his hair in pigtails and painted his nails pink.

But why do I think the joke's going to be on me this time?

by Poppy

Oh dear. I was right. **Sigh**. As soon as the programme had finished, Molly rushed upstairs. I went with her, of course. We go EVERYWHERE together. **Woof. Woof**. Although sometimes, like now, I wish we didn't.

Charlie always comes too. He pretends it's because Molly's bed is more comfortable than the armchair downstairs. But I know it's because he can't bear to be left out. **Wag. Wag**.

Molly is hunting through the drawers under her bed. She finds what she's looking for – her book of make-its that she found in a charity shop.

Oh no. This is what I was dreading. There's a chapter on **Things To Make Your Pet . . .**

ANIMAL PRINT SHOULDER BAG

Keep all of your pet's toys tidy in this funky bag.

Get ready!

Ruler or tape measure, scissors, 2 pieces of animal print fabric in 20cm squares, straight pins, needle and thread (get a colour that matches your fabric), pencil, 1 metre of wide decorative ribbon, 40cm of ribbon with beaded fringe

Note: All the make-its in this book can be made with a sewing machine – if you have one!

Step-by-step

1. Place the two 20cm squares of fabric together, print side facing in. Pin together along three of the edges.

2. Start sewing 1.5cm down from one corner along the three pinned edges, approximately 5mm in from the edge. You may want to draw a straight line with a pencil to guide you as you sew. Take out the pins as you go. When you reach the end of the third side, tie a strong knot at the end of the stitching. Cut off any excess thread.

3. Leaving the two sewn squares with the print side in, fold over 1.5cm of fabric along the unsewn top edges of the bag. Pin these flaps down and sew along the edges as you did in step 2. When you reach the end, tie a knot and cut off the excess thread.

4. Decide on the length of your shoulder strap. You can do this by pinning the ribbon to the top of the bag and trying it on to see where the bag falls when you wear it.

5. When you've got the right length, cut the ribbon about 2.5cm longer than you want it to be. Fold over 1.5cm at one end of the ribbon. Pin this end inside one side of the bag, centring it over the seam. Sew across the ribbon twice and tie it off with a knot. Repeat this step with the other end of the ribbon.

Make sure the ribbon is not twisted before you start sewing, and make sure both ends of the ribbon are sewn directly across from each other so that your strap will fall evenly.

6. Turn the bag right side out.

7. Take one edge of the beaded fringe ribbon, and place it along the bottom edge of the finished bag. Pin the entire length of the ribbon along the bottom edge. Using a running stitch, sew along the centre of the ribbon until the entire bottom is covered. Be sure to take out the pins as you sew. Knot the thread and cut off the excess.

8. Congratulate yourself on making this fabulous fashion accessory!

***Note:** If you don't want to sew this bag, you can use glue along all the edges that require stitching. This includes the seams of the bag, the ribbon handle and the beaded fringe along the bottom.*

FRIENDSHIP BRACELETS

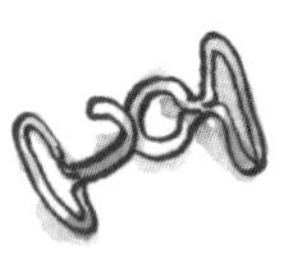

Show your dog just how much you love him by making matching friendship bracelets for both of you!

Get ready!

Tape measure, craft foam, pencil, scissors, glue, ribbon, small hook-and-loop fastener tape with peel-and-stick backing.

Take your pick!

Sequins, buttons or beads
Sewing needle and thread

Step-by-step

1. Use the tape measure to measure your wrist and your dog's paw to see how long your bracelets need to be. Add about 2.5cm to that measurement and mark it on your foam sheet. Hold the sheet up to your wrist/paw and decide how wide you want your bracelet to be. Mark the width on the bracelet and cut it. Re-check the fit and cut off any excess length. You should have a little overlap at the ends.

2. The width of your ribbon should be narrower than the width of your bracelet. The ribbon's length should be the same length as the bracelet. Hold the ribbon next to the bracelet and cut the ribbon to the correct size.

3. Carefully glue the ribbon to the centre of the bracelet. Allow the glue to dry completely. Re-glue any loose edges.

4. Take one 'loop' piece of hook-and-loop tape and press it near one end on the front of the bracelet. Turn the bracelet over and stick a 'hook' piece on the back of the opposite side of the bracelet. To be extra sure they stick, you might want to glue or sew them into position.

5. Choose sequins, buttons or beads to decorate your bracelet. Experiment with your design until you love the look. Glue the decorations in place, or use a needle and thread to sew on buttons and beads. Let everything dry and settle on a flat surface overnight before wearing your bracelet or fastening it carefully around your dog's paw.

Word of caution: Some dogs don't like to wear jewellery. If your dog tries to chew off the bracelet, it is best to remove it for his own safety. There's no accounting for taste!

DYNAMIC COLLAR

Your dog will look dashing in this designer collar – designed by you!

Get ready!

Nylon dog collar, ribbons (same width as the collar), tape measure or ruler, hook-and-loop fastener tape with peel-and-stick backing, scissors, clear nail varnish, a nail

Step-by-step

1. Measure the collar from end to end. Cut a piece of ribbon 7.5cm longer than your measurement and apply clear nail varnish to the ends to keep them from unravelling. Allow to dry.

2. Hook-and-loop tape comes in strips, one for the 'hook' side and one for the loop side. Cut small pieces of the tape to match the width of your collar.

3. Stick one of the 'loop' pieces about 2.5cm in from the buckle and another about 2.5cm in from the end. Add 'loop' pieces every 7.5cm to 10cm in between on the smooth side of the collar.

4. Turn the collar over and put one 'loop' piece about 5cm to 7.5cm in from the end of the collar, then turn the collar back over.

5. Set the ribbon, wrong side up beside the collar and attach one 'hook' piece of tape to the wrong side of the ribbon to match each 'loop' piece on the collar, including the one on the other side near the end of the collar.

6. Wait a few hours to make sure the hook-and-loop tape is firmly stuck to the collar and ribbon, then attach the ribbon by connecting the hook-and-loop pieces together.

7. You'll need to use a nail or another sharp object to poke holes in the ribbon in the spots where the collar has holes. If the holes close up (this happens with some ribbon), you can cut a slightly larger hole with scissors and apply clear nail varnish around its edges.

LUXURY FUR-LINED DOG BED

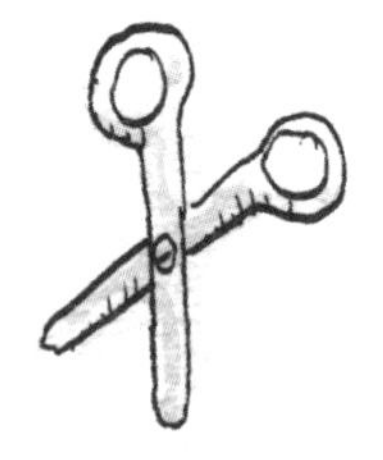

Every dog loves to sleep and your dog will adore this comfy bed.

Get ready!

1.2m x 60cm of fake fur, 40cm x 60cm of any other thick fabric, scissors, large needle and thread, old bath towel, pins, marker, and a 30-40cm round foam circle (for the bed's base).

Note: ***if you have a large dog, you need more fabric and a bigger foam circle.***

Step-by-step

1. Using the marker, draw around the foam circle at one end of each piece of fabric. Now cut out the two circles, leaving an extra 2cm all round for a hem.

2. Pin the circles together, fur side facing in, and then sew all around, leaving a 15cm gap. Take out the pins as you sew.

3. Turn the circles inside out so the fur is showing. Stuff the foam circle inside and sew up the gap. This is the bed's base.

4. From the remaining fur fabric, cut two 75 x 30cm rectangles. Sew them together at one short end and fold lengthwise, fur side facing in. Sew along the length and turn right side out, so you have a long 1.5m x 15cm furry tube. This will form the sides of your dog bed.

5. Fold the towel until it fits snugly inside the tube.

6. Wrap the tube around the circular pillow so there are no gaps. Then pin and sew the edges together.

7. Sew the the pillow and the sides together to finish off the bed!

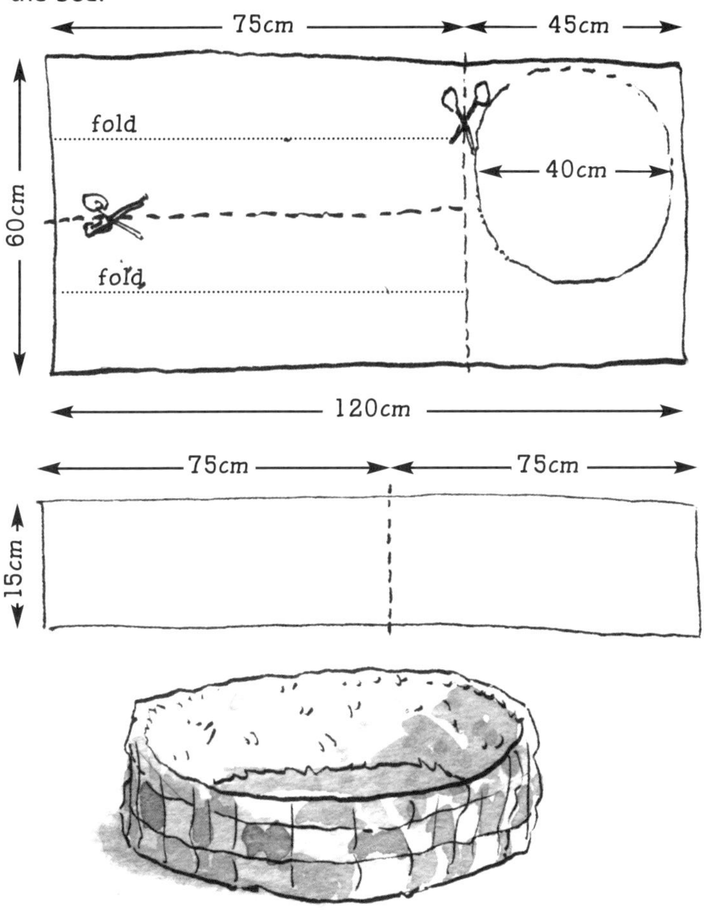

Me and **Charlie** hide under the bed and try not to catch Molly's eye while she makes her mind up what to make.

She decides on the dog bed. **Phew oh phew!** She is so busy that she doesn't even realise it's lunchtime. Her mum has to call her. TWICE!!

Meanwhile, I am practically fainting from hunger. I haven't eaten anything for at least an hour! I try eating a few of the shiny buttons in Molly's sewing box. They taste all plasticky and horrid. I spit them out again.

DOUBLE YUCK!!

The funniest part of all this though is that Molly is going to ask her gran to knit **Charlie** a sweater. **Hee hee**. I can't wait to see his face when she makes him wear it. The thought makes me laugh so much I fall off the bed.

Chapter Four

Molly says we are going WALKIES to the fair! I LOVE walkies! They are great!

Thump! Thump!

Molly puts on my lead and then we are OUTSIDE! I am happy. Wag. Wag. This is so GREAT!

We walk across the park. There is a puddle. Hurray, I love puddles! Jump! Splash! Shake my fur! Shake. Shake. BIG shake! Molly is really cross. Oops!

The fair is so exciting! I'll be able to see Mavis. Hurrah. Hurrah.

Ooh, I can smell food. Lots and lots and lots of food. **Yum, yum, bum scrum!** Molly wants to go on the rides. Loads of rides. They look SCARY to me! Molly tells me to sit. Sitting is boring. I can smell food. Mouthwatering, delicious, SCRUMMY food! My tummy is making noises. It sounds like **Bernie** when he is very cross. **Grrr grrr.**

I sniff around. There are bits of food EVERYWHERE! Just dropped on the ground. **Sniff. Sniff.** I don't know where to start.

Mmmm, mmmm, mmmmm!

Hot dogs. **Slurp.**
Candy floss. **Double slurp.**
Doughnuts. Dribble.
Ice cream. **Gulp**.
And Chips!

I feel a bit sick. **Sigh**.

I can see Molly in the queue. It is very, very long. Boring.

Time to explore and see if I can find **MaViS**. OK, concentrate. Hang on! **Sniff. Sniff.** **Mmmmm!** A bit of sausage dropped on the floor. **Slurp!**

That's better!

I head into a small tent. **Oh** it's very dark in here. There are lots of candles. They smell funny. **ACHOOO!** They make me sneeze.

I can see scarves. **Lots** of them. Everywhere! They are on chairs, tables and hanging from the ceiling. I would like to play with them, but I think Molly would be cross. **Sigh**. There is a funny smell. **Sniff. Sniff.** Friendly, but musky. I am a bit nervous.

'Tooonііііііght the mooooon is in Veeenuuuusss,' says a voice.

I look round.

'I said, the mooooon tooonііііііght is in Veeenuuuusss.'

Boy oh boy, whose voice is THAT? I sniff and blink through the dark and the scarves. **Sniff. Sniff.** **Blink. Blink.**

I can just make out the shape of another dog. She is very upright and elegant, and is wearing a scarf tied round her ears. **Hee hee.** She looks funny. **Wag. Wag.**

The funny-dressed dog comes a bit closer. **Sniff. Sniff.** I smell her. I don't believe it. It's **MaViS!** She hasn't recognised me. I think all the perfumed candles and scarves must be playing havoc with her nose. **Wag. Wag.** **MaViS** starts to speak again.

'Hellooooooooooo! I'm **MaViS**, the Mystic Mutt. I have been trrrained to use my psyyychic powers and read the staaaars by Stellaaaaa the Foooortune Teller. She's taaaaaaaught me everything! I can tell yoooooooou ANYTHING yoooooooou want toooo knoooooow.'

I can't stand it any more. **MaViS's** new voice is very annoying.

'Er, **MaViS**, it's me, **Poppy**.'

MaViS sniffs through the darkness, coming so close her whiskers tickle my nose. Then she sits back happily on her haunches.

'**Cor blimey**, if it isn't little **Poppy**. Well I never. But why didn't you say so, treacle?

'You must have thought I was a right doughnut.'

I scratch behind my ear to hide my smile. 'Er, why WERE you talking in that voice, **Mavis**?'

'It's good for business, ducks. Since Stella adopted me, I've learnt everyfink there is to know about astrology. Problem is, no dog takes me serious-like if I talk in me normal voice, so I came up with the idea of **Mystic Mutt**. It went down a treat and I ain't looked back since, Popster, I can tell you.'

Mavis winks at me, 'Mind you, ducks, remembering to talk in my maaarvellooous mystic voice is a right pain in the bum sometimes.'

I **love Mavis**. She hasn't changed at all. **Wag. Wag.**

Mavis wasn't joking when she told me she's learnt loads about astrology. **Wowzer!** Are star signs interesting! **Mavis** has written it all down and hopes to have it published one day. She's given me the first draft to read . . .

Mystic Mutt's Star Signs for Canines

Aries

March 21 to April 20

Favourite Place: The local park

Favourite Food: Sausages

The Aries dog is adventurous and energetic, always exploring new areas. Aries mutts love to go for walks and their pioneering nature leads them in new directions. Their confidence and impulsiveness sometimes gets them into trouble, whether it's following a rabbit down a hole or a stick into a pond. But the Aries dog will always happily launch himself into another adventure, especially if it's with that little mutt from across town that always knows where to find the tastiest sausages.

Best Owners: Pisces, Capricorn

Taurus

April 21 to May 20

Favourite Place:
Dozing in front of the fire

Favourite Food:
Anything rabbit-flavoured

Taurus dogs are loving and cuddly. They are also patient and reliable, happily putting up with their owner's habits and strange ways. The Taurus dog loves nothing better than spending time one-to-one with his owner and can be very jealous of anyone who dares to interrupt that special time. But mostly, Taurus dogs are quiet and peaceful and like everything around them to be happy and secure. They're also happiest when there's a bone nearby and they are curled up in front of a warm fire.

Best Owners: Capricorn, Aries

Gemini

May 21 to June 21

Favourite Place:
The garden

Favourite Food: Liver

Gemini dogs are very lively and are happy practically anywhere doing anything. They love sharing things with their owner, especially things they've found - like an old boot they've dug up in the garden. No matter how old they are, Gemini dogs are always youthful and have a cheeky sense of humour. They also have a bit of a mischievous streak, and they find covering their owners with water when they get out of the bath, or burying car keys in the back garden very funny indeed.

Best Owners: Aquarius, Libra

Cancer

June 22 to July 22

Favourite Place: Curled up in their bed

Favourite Food: Gravy

Cancer dogs are protective and caring. They are very emotional and perceptive – they know what's on their owner's mind even before the owner does. Cancer dogs are sensitive and tender. They're also the most sympathetic of all dogs, understanding instinctively what their owners feel.

Best Owners: Pisces, Aries, Capricorn

Leo

July 23 to August 22

Favourite Place: Anywhere that involves walkies

Favourite Food: Bones

Leo dogs are strong and faithful. They are energetic and enthusiastic, throwing themselves into every activity, whether it's running through a field or fetching a ball. They even sleep with gusto - their snores can make the walls vibrate! Leo dogs think that they are masters of all they survey and always act like the boss. Above all, Leo dogs are loyal to their owners - until they spot a squirrel.

Best Owners: Virgo, Pisces, Aries

Virgo

August 23 to September 22

Favourite Place:
Their basket

Favourite Food:
Doggie treats

Virgo dogs are modest and a little shy. While they know they are the best-looking dogs in the neighbourhood, they hate showing off.

Virgo dogs are also reliable and obedient. Given a task, they carry it out fully and faithfully but turn bashful whenever praised (unless there are doggie treats on offer). Virgo dogs are happiest lying in the sun, watching their family play.

Best Owners: Leo, Libra

Libra

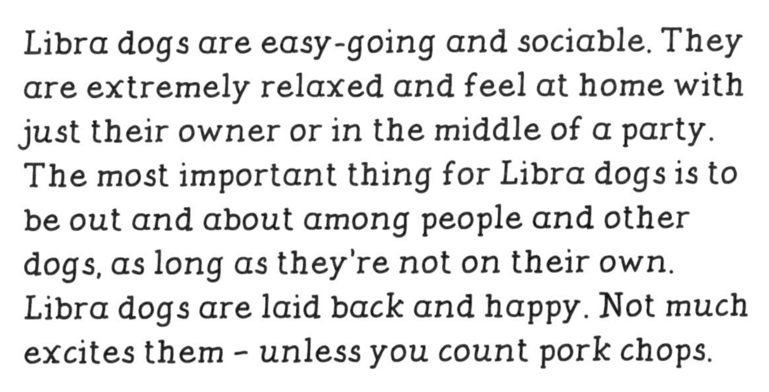

September 23 to October 23

Favourite Place:
The lounge

Favourite Food:
Peanut butter

Libra dogs are easy-going and sociable. They are extremely relaxed and feel at home with just their owner or in the middle of a party. The most important thing for Libra dogs is to be out and about among people and other dogs, as long as they're not on their own. Libra dogs are laid back and happy. Not much excites them - unless you count pork chops.

Best Owners: Leo, Sagittarius

Scorpio

October 24 to November 21

Favourite Place: *Looking out of the window*

Favourite Food: *Bacon*

Scorpio dogs are determined and focused, always accomplishing whatever they set their minds to. They are also passionate and forceful dogs, relishing every activity and often have so much fun they end up lying on the floor panting with exhaustion. They can be very intense and have been known to stare at squirrels through the window for hours at a time without moving. Unless it's dinner time, of course.

Best Owners: Capricorn, Sagittarius

Sagittarius

November 22 to December 21

Favourite Place: *Anywhere outside*

Favourite Food: Cake

Sagittarius dogs are carefree and freedom-loving. They love wide open spaces and can't wait to explore them. They are happy and good-natured dogs who love to romp and play with their owners. Sagittarius dogs never hide how they feel because they are always happy and fun-loving. They are at their happiest when chasing a ball.

Best Owners: Capricorn, Aquarius

Capricorn

December 22 to January 19

Favourite Place: The kitchen

Favourite Food: Anything gourmet

Capricorn dogs are patient and careful. They believe that good things come to dogs who wait, so they are content to sit quietly by their owner's feet at mealtimes.

They are very particular dogs, sleeping in a certain place, with the same toys, and resisting any diversion from their usual route during walkies. Capricorn dogs are disciplined, except when it comes to fridge-raiding.

Best Owners: Taurus, Scorpio, Cancer

Aquarius

January 20 to February 18

Favourite Place: Lazing in the sun

Favourite Food: Turkey

Aquarius dogs are friendly and loyal. They stick by their owner's side while watching TV or lie under their owner's deck chair while sunbathing. Aquarius dogs can also be independent and inventive, often surprising their owners with new tricks. The Aquarius dog is a true friend in every sense - unless his owner should forget supper.

Best Owners: Sagittarius, Libra

Pisces

February 19 to March 20

Favourite Place: The car

Favourite Food: Ham

The Pisces dogs is kind and loving. They have a giving nature and are very caring. They make great rescue dogs and love nothing better than long drives in the car. Because of their unselfish nature they are easy-going to live with. They are easy to train and love to go for long walks. Especially if those long walks lead to a park.

Best Owners:
Cancer, Aries

Boy oh boy. **MaVIS** is one smart dog. Almost as smart as **Alfie**! **Woof. Woof.** She is **Greeeeeeeeeeeeeat**. Sorry, I meant **GREAT!**

Woof. Woof!

Just before Molly and I leave, **MaVIS** says something strange to me.

'You know what, darlin', I see much happiness in your future. A big house and lots and lots of pink.'

Hee hee. That **MaVIS**. Always mucking around. **Wag. Wag.**

She obviously hasn't seen Molly's dad's bank balance then. It's always in the red according to him. I reckon she's barking up the wrong tree (geddit!) with that prediction!

Wag. Wag.

Chapter Five

I am snoozing in my basket. Molly, Nathan and their parents have gone to Molly's friend Meenakshi's birthday party.

I **love** Meenakshi! She always brings lovely yummy doggie treats for me when she comes over. **Wag. Wag.** But today I have to stay at home. Molly says it isn't a puppy party. **Sigh.**

Charlie is snoring loudly on the sofa. He is a very noisy sleeper. **Wag. Wag.** I feel warm and dozy. **Mmm.** I LOVE snoozing. **Wag. Wag.**

I am dreaming of jumping into a swimming pool filled with onion gravy. **Mmmm!** I **LOVE** onion gravy. **Yum. Yum.**

Something taps me hard on the nose. **Tap. Tap. Tap**. Ow! That HURTS!

I am cross. I open one eye. **Wowzer!** A pigeon is sitting on the side of my basket!

Hello! Hello! Hi! Hi pigeon!
I jump up. The pigeon falls off the basket. **Oops!** Sorry!

Charlie stands up on the sofa. He crouches low like a hunter. He licks his lips. The pigeon looks scared! Poor pigeon!

I shake my head. Charlie licks his lips. Oh! **Bad** cat. **Bad bad** cat. You cannot eat the pigeon! He is our friend. **Woof. Woof.** Charlie shrugs and sits back down.

The pigeon blinks. He reaches under his wing with his beak and pulls out a letter.

A letter! **Oh wow, oh wow, oh wow!** I **love** letters! Who's it from? Who's it from?

Sniff. Sniff. Oooh, perfume! Expensive perfume!

TALLULAH!

Boy oh boy. Tallulah. She really is one in a million. I **love** her. She is great. And she makes me laugh. A lot. **Wag. Wag.**

After Tallulah left the London Dogs' Home, **Bernie** used to tell me Tallulah's story every night. It's a real life shaggy dog story. **Wag. Wag.**

Tallulah's Story

as told by Bernie

From the moment Tallulah turned up at the London Dogs' Home it was clear she was meant for better things. Well, Tallulah certainly thought so, anyway. She refused to walk on any concrete surface, afraid of scratching her delicate little paws. Instead, the staff had to carry her everywhere. She refused to eat unless a member of staff had cut up her food into tiny bite-size pieces. And she was not satisfied until her fur was groomed to a fine sheen and her favourite pink ribbon had been tied in a perfect bow around her neck. Quite honestly, if it were down to me, Tallulah would have been given a sharp nip on her pretty derrière, but everyone else seemed to think she was adorable. And as you know, Poppy, I'm not one to complain.

Even Tallulah's cage looked different from ours. Instead of newspaper, she had pages from ***Vogue*** and ***Vanity Fair*** lining her cage. Her litter tray was spotless and even her basket had a Harrod's blanket in it. It was made of the softest material I have ever felt in my life. 'Cashmere, sweetie,' she told me. 'Cashmere. You should try it.'

I mean, what would I be doing with cashmere? I ask you. Newspaper is fine by me – much more interesting.

Then one day her whole life changed when a real-life celebrity walked into the Home looking for a dog to adopt.

Every dog has its day, and that day belonged to Tallulah. She opened her puppy-dog eyes as wide as she could, pranced around her cage on her oh-so-pretty legs and yipped in what was obviously considered to be a cute and appealing fashion – although it made me feel quite sick!

The celebrity, an ex-member of one of the world's biggest girl groups, took one look and fell totally and utterly head-over-heels in love. Tallulah would probably have felt the same, but she was far too busy being in love with herself.

So off she went to live in Hampstead, until the singer decided to try her luck in Hollywood and the pair of them boarded a plane and flew off into the sunset. First class all the way, of course. All right for some! But as you know, Poppy, I'm not one to complain.

I love that story. It's a real-life fairy-tail!!
Hee hee.

Tallulah has always kept in touch.
She's great like that. **Wag. Wag.**

She is so smart. And RICH! **Wag. Wag.** She manages to persuade passing birds to fly the letters to England in return for all the peanuts they can eat. That's smart, huh? All kinds of birds turn up. We even had a stork once. **Hee hee.**

Boy oh boy, life with Tallulah as a friend is so exciting.

I can't wait to read the letter. What does she say? What does she say? **Woof. Woof.**

THE BIGGEST HOUSE
THE POSHEST STREET
THE SMARTEST AREA
LOS ANGELES
AMERICA

Ciao My Darling Poppy

I am writing this from the luxury of my very own dog chalet made from the finest hand-crafted pine. I am lounging on the most divine dog-sized Burberry bed. You would love it, Poppet. And just outside my door I can see my darling little picnic table which I can use whenever I feel like dining 'al fresco'. Although of course most of the time I eat at the table with Kerry, but it's important to have the option, don't you think?

Once I've finished writing this, it will be time to get dressed. Of course I have outfits for every occasion. A maid comes in the morning to help me choose and dress me.

I'm all on my own today. Kerry is off filming at some

tiresome film set. It must be such a bore. But of course she's made sure I've got everything I could possibly need. Nothing's too much trouble where little old me is concerned.

She's left a video playing so I don't get lonely. Doggie videos are all the rage in America, you know. It's so sweet. It shows my very own little doggie friend pottering around a garden, playing with toys and eating lunch. Absolutely adorable. I love it.

Next week, K has to go and promote her latest film in New York. Yawn! But there's no need to worry about me, I'm booked into the Ritzy Canine Carriage House Pet Hotel in New York. It's $250 a night, but it's worth every single penny (or dollar, I should say).

Of course I always stay in the Presidential Suite. The staff there are such darlings. They'll go to absolutely any lengths to make sure that my stay is an absolute delight. Upon my arrival I am greeted by my own personal chaperone who shows me around my suite so I can check everything is to the standard I have come to expect. Well, I do have a reputation as a celebrity's dog to protect, you know. It's such a relaxing place – you can have manicures, pedicures, hairstyling, ear cleaning, and there are the most heavenly relaxing massage sessions. I have my own minder to tuck me in at night and who makes sure all my gourmet meals are to my liking. Their Asian chicken stirfry is to die for. You'd adore it, sweetie darling. You really would. Absolute heaven.

I do hope all the old crowd will be there. Jennifer Lopez's cocker spaniel and corgi are such fun, and Harry, Gerri Halliwell's dog, is absolutely charming as well as being an incorrigible flirt. You know, last time I saw him, he couldn't stop commenting on the softness of my fur and how sweetly perfumed it smelt. Oh, he's such a one. So, so sweet!

Which, darling, brings me to the point of this letter. I wanted to get you a little trinket. Money is no object, sweetie, you know that. I've enclosed the latest Pampered Puppy catalogue so you can pick something. It's up to you, my darling girl. Simply select a little gift and send it back via the pigeon. He's a crusty old thing, I know, but he's very reliable.

Oh fiddlesticks. darling, I'm going to have to fly. My mobile phone is ringing. You should see it – it's so dinky and it clips straight on to my collar. Absolutely adorable. That will be K. She likes to ring me and talk to me down the phone. She worries I'll get lonely pottering around in this little old mansion on my ownsome. So sweet.

I've got to run, my angel. Take care. Millions of kisses.

Write soon.

Tallulah xxx

I look through the catalogue. **Wow oh wow oh wow.** All these things you can buy! I can't believe it. Just take a look . . .

pampered puppy

Here at Pampered Puppy we bring you the best features, shopping, guides and directory on the net. Just check out these latest products available for your little poppets. The must-have item this season is a summer house to keep your darling dog protected from that summer sun. And if you really love your dog, why not treat her to a new summer wardrobe. She'll love you for it!

DESIGNER COLLARS AND JEWELLERY

Candy-striped collar

For the fun-loving dog with a sense of style.

$24.00

order from www.barkspupavenue.com

Charm necklace

Made of the finest sterling silver, this necklace will make other dogs drool with envy.

$179.00

order from www.parkavenuepaws.com

Faux Pearl Necklace

As seen in the movie How to Lose a Guy in 10 Days!

Available in four sizes

$95.00–$105.00

order from www.barkspupavenue.com

the ultimate resource for your pampered pooch

www.pamperedpuppy.net

HANDCRAFTED PET CARRIERS

For dogs who love to be treated like royalty, check out a range of truly chic carriers – the perfect fashion accessory!

from $80.00

order from www.barkspupavenue.com

OUTERWEAR

Denim Duds

Designer wear for casual dog days, with matching hair bows.

$44.99

order from www.barkspupavenue.com

Dogball hat

Perfect park wear for your pup. It's a steal at . .

$14.99

order from www.barkspupavenue.com

pampered puppy

PARTY WEAR

Black suit

For those formal occasions when you want your dog to be smart and sassy.

$59.99-$69.99

order from www.parkavenuepaws.com

The ultimate party dress

Your dog will be the belle of the ball in this elegant party dress. Available in two colours.

$195.00

order from www.barkspupavenue.com

The Audrey Hepbone

Formal wear for the glamour pooch. A crystal tiara with hot pink bone and pale pink feather boa. To die for, darling!

$46.00

order from www.barkspupavenue.com

Zsa Zsa Feather Boa

It's outrageous! It's huge! It makes your pooch look like a star.

$14.99

order from www.barkspupavenue.com

the ultimate resource for your pampered pooch

www.pamperedpuppy.net

BEDS

The Victorian

This elaborate wrought-iron bed will ensure that your dog never wants to sleep on your bed again!

One of many styles available.

from $250.00

order from www.callingalldogs.com

FEEDERS

Raised feeders

Made of the finest fossil stone with pewter paws, these feeders mean that your dog never has to stoop again!

$240.00–$499.00

order from www.barkspupavenue.com

GIFTS

Treat machine

Watch your dog push the handle to get a treat!

$49.94

order from www.barkspupavenue.com

PET WEDDINGS

Are your pets inseparable? Then give them a day they will never forget on a sunset beach in Hawaii. Our full marriage service will cement their love forever!

www.beachwed.com/pets/index.html

pampered puppy 

SUMMER HOUSES

The Little Mary

This bright and elegant tent with delicate French tassels and pom-pom is a house fit for a queen.

$175.00

order from www.callingalldogs.com

The Guinevere

Made from rich tapestry fabric and lined with velvet, this tent guarantees your pet magical dreams.

$195.00

order from www.callingalldogs.com

HANDSOME HOMES

The ultimate in dog houses, handmade by skilled craftsmen!

Prices on application

order from www.lapetitemaison.com

Wowzer! What a life. Isn't she just the luckiest dog in the world? **Woof. Woof.**

I feel a bit sad though. I wish I could see Tallulah again.

I must write her a letter back. I know what I would like more than anything else in the world – a proper home for **Bernie**, but you can't order that from a catalogue.

Wow oh wow oh wow. I have an idea! If **Bernie** has his own house, maybe his size won't be such a problem. Then, maybe, just maybe, things will work out fine. **Wow oh wow** Tallulah is just the person to help me.

Oh, I can hear Molly running to the front door. Tallulah's life sounds great, but I wouldn't swap my Molly for anything. Not even for the biggest pile of **doggie choc drops** in the world.

Uh uh. No way. No sir! **Woof. Woof.**

Chapter Six

Woof! Woof! How excited am I? It's the dead of night, Molly and her family are all upstairs fast asleep. I can hear Molly's dad snoring from here! Snore! Snore! ***Tee hee!*** He's so NOISY! Mind you, he's not as noisy as Charlie who is munching his favourite cheese and onion crisps in my ear. LOUDLY.

It's pouring with rain outside and there's thunder and lightning!

Crash! Bang!

I don't like it. So Charlie and I are going to watch videos so I won't be frightened any more! Wag. Wag.

And even better, I'm going to tell you all about them . . .

Wag. Wag.

Lady And The Tramp.
I liked this film. It was good. Lady was very pretty. She was nice. It was good.

Oh, for goodness' sake!
It's Charlie here!
I've decided to take over because:
a) Poppy's fallen asleep.
b) And as you can see from what she's written, if she carries on with her reviews – well, quite frankly, it'll be rubbish.

Right. Here goes...

Lady And The Tramp

Lady, a well-bred King Charles spaniel (if you like that kind of thing), is displaced by a new arrival in her home (a human baby, urgh!) and blamed when she accidentally knocks over the baby's cradle chasing a tasty fat rat out of the nursery. She runs away and falls in with tough street-mongrel Tramp. On her way home after a magical evening, she is thrown into the dog pound. Her adventures are only just beginning.

Best bit is when the shifty Siamese cats sing: *We Are Siamese If You Please*. Brilliant! Skip the ending, it's really soppy (unless you like soppy, of course!)

Charlie Rating: Three cat paws (out of my four)

Dog Of Flanders

Nello and his grandfather find an injured dog and nurse it back to health, calling it Patraasche after Nello's mother. Nello is fascinated by art, and befriends Alois, a girl with similar interests. But tragedy soon sets in. It's one of the saddest stories ever and not for the faint-hearted – even I had to wipe away a tear.

Charlie Rating: Three cat paws

Cats And Dogs

Now this is more like it. A film about world domination by cats! Lou (a beagle) is an inexperienced dog-agent who is accidentally assigned to protect a professor working on a serum to cure an allergy to dogs. But evil cat-mastermind Mr Tinkles plans to steal the serum and alter it, creating a virus that will make *everyone* allergic to dogs (his plan rocks!!!) and make cats

the rulers of the world. Done with real animals and people, and clever animal-tronics.

The best bit is the ninja Siamese cats – they know kung fu and aren't afraid to use it!

Charlie Rating: Four cat paws

Oliver And Company

Oliver the orphaned cat meets a group of stray dogs led by the Artful Dodger. He is adopted by a human girl, Jenny, but her pedigree cat, Georgette, gets jealous. Kidnapped by the evil Sykes, Oliver must rely on his new-found friends to save the day.

The best bit is Dodger's musical number, *Why Should I Worry?* And look out for a Mickey Mouse watch (it's a Disney film!).

Charlie Rating: Two cat paws

101 Dalmatians (animated film)

When human beings Roger and Anita fall in love and get married, their dogs do too! Dalmatians Pongo and Perdita have fifteen cute little puppies, but the dogs are stolen by

the henchmen of Cruella De Vil, an evil woman who wants a coat made of Dalmatian fur. The dogs rescue their offspring, along with 84 other stolen puppies.

Watch out for . . . Mickey Mouse outlines hidden in the Dalmatians' spots and windows (yep, another Disney film!).

Charlie Rating: Four cat paws

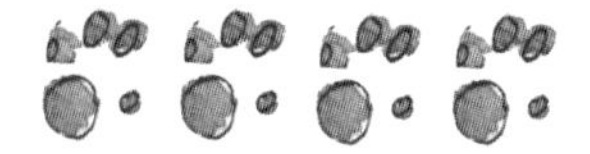

101 Dalmatians (live-action)

When human beings Roger and Anita fall in love and get married . . . hang on . . . yes, this is a remake of the animated film, but done with real people and real dogs (must have been a nightmare!!).

Charlie Rating: Two cat paws. Not as good as the original.

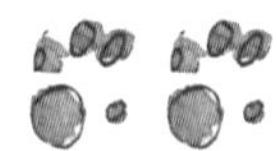

102 Dalmatians (live-action)

After the events of *101 Dalmatians*, Cruella De Vil has been cured! Now a dog-lover, she is released from prison, and takes over a run-down dog sanctuary. But Cruella doesn't stay good for long – the chimes of Big Ben restore her to her old self. Now she wants 99

Dalmatians to make a coat, and three more for a hood. But Dipstick the dog, one of the original puppies, now with puppies of his own, is determined to stop her . . . with a little human help.

Listen out for . . . Waddlesworth, a stupid parrot who thinks he's a Rottweiler, but can translate between the dogs and the humans.

Charlie Rating: Two cat paws

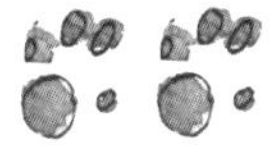

Beethoven

Canine comedy about a dog-hating dad, George Newton, stuck with a cute little St Bernard puppy that soon grows into a giant disaster area! He smashes crockery, bites off sensitive parts, and everything is chaos. The dog's already peed on someone before the opening credits have finished – so you know it can only get funnier.

Ask yourself . . . what kind of alarm system has lasers, but doesn't notice when you shower it with broken glass?

Charlie Rating: Three cat paws

Beethoven's 2nd

Just as funny as the original, except that now Beethoven is a dad.

Watch out for ... Beethoven pulling the side off a house. Also watch the girl whose tickets Beethoven retrieves from a bully – she starts off with her hair in a pony-tail, which then disappears!

Charlie Rating: Three cat paws

Beethoven's 3rd

Nowhere near as good as the other two.

Watch out for ... Beethoven's meeting with a skunk, and an important lesson for boys who have a secret love of Hello Kitty.

Fast-forward to ... whenever the dog is on screen – which isn't very often.

Charlie Rating: One cat paw

Benji

Benji is a stray dog who lives in a big, deserted house all alone. Each morning he leaves the house, has a chat with a friendly policeman, chases the same cat and visits the same family for his breakfast, where he is fussed over by two children. When the children are kidnapped and taken to Benji's big house, Benji saves the day. There's even romance for him along the way. Benji is a pretty cool and clever dog, but it is super-soppy in places.

Watch out for ... a new Benji coming out soon.

Charlie Rating: Two cat paws

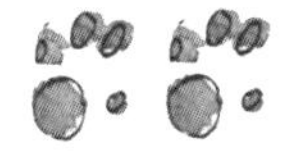

Babe

OK, so this is about a pig, not a dog. But Babe is a pig who THINKS he's a dog. This is a brilliant film – really funny – and it has a great ending where Babe wins the County Sheepdog Trials. There's a fantastically wicked cat, too. I could watch this again and again.

Watch out for ... the little singing mice.

Charlie Rating: Four cat paws

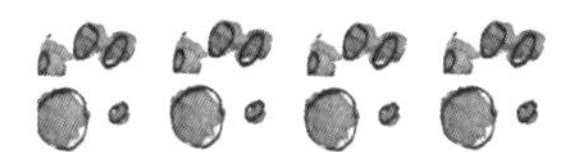

Chapter Seven

by Poppy

Hurrah! Hurrah! Woof! Woof!
Today I got another letter from **Bernie!**
Wag! Wag!

I **love** him! So much. He's super-dooper-pooper-scooper-fan-waggy-tastically **GREAT!**

Thump! Thump!

He manages to send me letters from the London Dogs' Home without anyone knowing. Yep, that's how smart he is!
Wow oh wow!

Then I have to be extra clever to get them without being noticed. Boy oh boy, am I smart!

The lady from the London Dogs' Home comes to check on me to make sure I am being fed. Lots. And that I have a nice bed to sleep in. And that my fur is shiny and my tongue and eyes are brightedy-bright.

Wag, Wag,

She's very nice. I like her smell. Sniff. Sniff. **Mmmmm.** Friendly. Not as nice as Molly's though. **Wag. Wag.**

The lady bends over and pats me. Pat. Pat. **Pant. Pant.** I like her. She is NICE.

I wag my tail happily and wait till she is talking to Molly's mum and drinking a cup of tea. Then, quiet oh so quiet, I creep, creep, creep up to her coat. Very quiet, sssh!

A quick look round to check no one's watching. **Phew!** Coast is clear! I bury my nose in her pocket.

Sniff. Sniff. **Mmmmmm.** Gum drops and peppermints. Don't mind if I do! Scrummy!

Slurp. Slurp. Crunch. Crunch.

YUM!

Oops! Wag. Wag. Mustn't forget what I'm looking for. **Woof, Woof.** Here it is! Tucked away in a secret hole in the lining. A special letter. For me! From **Bernie**! Wag, Wag,

Nobody sees me. Apart from Charlie. Charlie and I have a cunning plan. If anyone does notice me, he is ready to cause a distraction by running up the curtains! Tee hee! Aren't we clever!

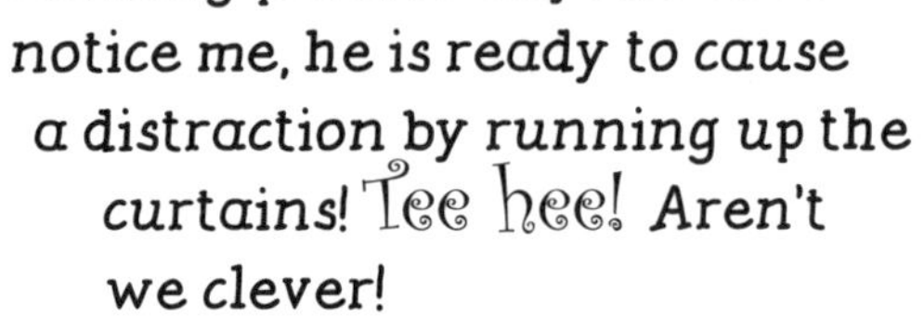

Quickly I pad over to my basket and drop the letter under my cushion. I **love** my cushion. It has **POPPY** in big colourful letters across it, just like my bowl. It's great. Wag. Wag.

I will read the letter later after Molly and her mum and dad have gone to bed.

Later that night...

Everyone is tucked up in bed. I can hear Molly's dad snoring. **SNORE! SNORE! SNOOOOOOOOORE!**

Sometimes it sounds as if the whole house is going to collapse. **Wag. Wag.** It is FUNNY!

Now I can read **Bernie's** letter. **Wag. Wag.** I pad into the kitchen and prop open the fridge door with my tail. The fridge light is great to read by...

Dear Poppy

I hope you are well. I'm fine. I am scratching a lot. I think I might have fleas. The cold draught is doing my back no good at all either. But like I always say, I can't complain.

There is very little to do here now that you have all gone. So I am still reading all the newspapers that line my cage. I know you love real-life stories, so I have ripped out all the ones that I think you would like to put into your scrapbook – if it's not too dog-eared! (I know it's an old joke. I don't get out much to learn new ones, but like I said, I can't complain.)

Reading all these stories has made me realise that I am very lucky (if you don't count the fleas and the cold draught). There are a lot of bad things that can happen if you are out in the real world. Not that I would know – it's a long time since I've been out there, but I can't complain.

I'm sorry this is just a short note, but I heard Mrs Pinkett say she is going to visit you shortly, so I have to make sure I am ready to slip this into her pocket without her noticing. I do it when she bends down to pat me on the way out. I hope she scratches me behind my ears – the fleas are biting me particularly badly there, I think.

Take good care of yourself, Poppy.

Best wishes,
Your good friend,

Bernie

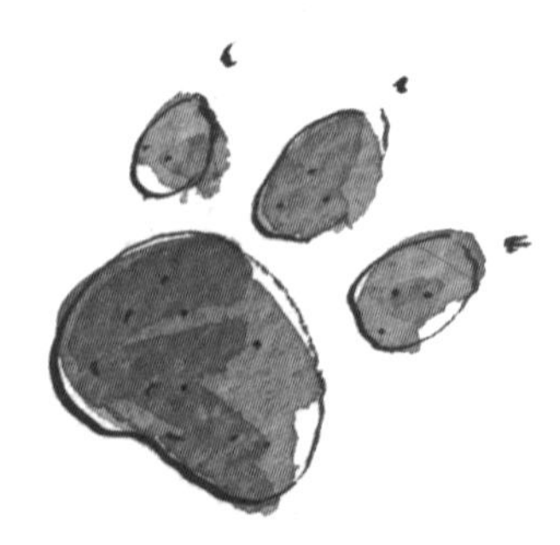

Poor **Bernie**. I wish someone as nice as Molly would adopt him, so he could be as happy as me. Sigh.

I pick up the letter and the cuttings in my mouth.

Trot trot, pad, pad back to my basket. Sssh. Sssh. Quietly I pull out my scrapbook from my secret hiding place.

Wow oh wow oh wow. I **LOVE** these stories. Not as much as I **LOVE Bernie** though. I miss him. Thinking about him makes me sad.

But these stories are GREAT. Even better than ham. And I **LOVE** ham. **Wag. Wag**

BRAVE DOG ATTACKS BEAR

by our America correspondent

An ordinary morning jog would have ended in tragedy if it hadn't been for the brave actions of a family dog.

As Bonnie Pankiw was running in a secluded part of Gaineau Park, near Meech Lake in America, accompanied by her nine-year-old Labrador, Queenie, they came face to face with an extremely fierce black bear. The bear charged straight at Bonnie to attack her. Queenie didn't hesitate – she leapt at the bear's hind legs, stopping the bear in its tracks. The bear came back more than once, trying to get around the dog to attack Bonnie. But each time, Queenie sprang into action, defending Bonnie and eventually managing to scare the bear away.

DOG SURVIVES HORRIFIC FALL

by our England correspondent

Sheba the springer spaniel plummeted over a 250ft cliff while chasing a seagull and miraculously survived without a scratch!

Owner, Tim Castle, watched in horror as his 11-month-old pet raced towards the edge when he took her for a walk along the cliffs at Beachy Head in Sussex.

He said, 'Sheba was so excited. She leapt out of the car as soon as I opened the door. My heart lurched when she went over. I thought that was it.'

A very distressed Tim drove to the police station where the coastguard was alerted. They were stunned to discover the dog completely unhurt and bounding along the shingle at the bottom of the cliff.

Coastguard, Colin Mulvana said, 'What must have saved her was the fact that the tide was in. She may have fallen into the water and then clambered on to the shore.

Tim said, 'She's a completely mad dog, always leaping off walls without looking.'

HE'S DOG-GONE FIT

by our sports correspondent

Owner, Fiona Foreman, was prevented from taking daily walks with her Jack Russell terrier by footpath closures. So she took her four-legged friend to the gym and put him on a treadmill for a work-out. Now the 12-year-old mutt enjoys work-outs at least two or three days a week. Fiona said, 'I was really worried when I saw 'KEEP OUT' signs going up all over the place because Jack is very active and needs his exercise. But perhaps it was a blessing in disguise, because he used to wear me out – whereas after a gym work-out, he's as zonked as I am!

IT'S A DOG'S LIFE

by our Italy correspondent

A stray dog in Italy, a five-year-old Husky called Sadu, won the hearts of ticket inspectors, and indeed the whole nation, to earn himself a free railway pass.

Every morning Sadu would board a train from Ostia Antic to make the 15-mile journey into Rome. At first the train inspector thought he must belong to someone on the train. Soon he realised that the dog was a stray. But where was he going every day? The inspector decided to follow the dog. He followed Sadu to a bakery where he stopped for a special biscuit. Then he went on to a local restaurant where he was given a lunch-time bowl of pasta. The inspector found out from the people who worked there that Sadu came every day. So impressed by the dog's cheeky lifestyle, he persuaded the train authorities to issue him with a free pass, and, Sadu became famous.

ELMO THE HERO

by our Canada correspondent

April 5, 1999, was no ordinary day for nine-year-old Ethan Beattie and his eight-year-old friend, Steven Murray. Ethan and Steven spent the early afternoon playing in a fort they had built in the woods across from Steven's farm, while Steven's dog, Elmo, lay uninterested nearby.

Later, joined by three other children, the group of boys headed to a pond to hunt for frogs, with Elmo in tow. After a couple of hours, Ethan and Steven decided it was time to head home.

The adventurous pair, along with Elmo, followed a trail they believed led back to the fort. However, the path they were following led them into very treacherous terrain, consisting of swamp, quicksand and other extremely dangerous waterways.

Lost and frightened, Ethan became entangled in brush and swamp and was unable to move. A terrified Steven ventured off in search of help. Eventually emerging from the woods, wet up to his shoulders and shivering from the cold, Steven frantically made his way home, but was unable to remember exactly where Ethan was.

Ethan remained in the woods, scared, wet and lost, but not alone. Sensing Ethan's fear, Elmo remained faithfully by Ethan's side providing warmth and comfort.

The boys' parents alerted the authorities. Almost immediately a huge search was underway but with no sign of Ethan as night fell, the search and rescue team contemplated calling off the rescue efforts until the next morning. In one final attempt before darkness set in, a firefighter saw a pair of eyes reflected in his torch light. A shivering Elmo and a nearly unconscious Ethan were discovered.

Suffering from severe hypothermia, Ethan was rushed to hospital, where he made a full recovery – thanks to Elmo!

SEPTEMBER 11TH SURVIVORS' TALES

by our New York correspondent

Eduardo Rivera, a blind computer operator, was on the 70th floor of the World Trade Center on September 11th, when terrorists deliberately flew a passenger airliner straight into the twin towers. Eduardo ordered his guide dog to leave without him, but the devoted Labrador battled through the flames and braved the growing panic to lead Eduardo safely down the stairs.

Another blind man, Mike Hingson, 51, was led to safety from the 78th floor by Roselle his Golden Labrador. It took half an hour to walk down to the ground floor.

'We smelled a lot of jet fuel on the way down,' said Hingson. 'Roselle never hesitated. She never panicked.'

In January 2002, both guide dogs were honoured by the British Guide Dogs for the Blind Association.

DOG FEED DOG

By our America correspondent

In Espanola, New Mexico, a German shepherd called Ranger cared for a dog trapped underneath an old abandoned camper van for nine days.

A passing neighbour watched ten-year-old Ranger crawl out from underneath the van, get a mouthful of snow and then carefully crawl back under the van to the stray dog, whose leg was caught in an animal trap. The neighbour was still unaware there was another dog and offered Ranger some food. Ranger carefully took the bowl in his mouth and carried it to the injured dog, barking at the neighbour to follow him. The story of Ranger and the stray dog spread throughout Espanola and more than 35 families offered to adopt the stray female, whose leg had to be amputated. Ranger became a big celebrity and remained the pride and joy of his owner, Leo Martinez.

From the archives

FINDING PRIVATE BROWN

by our history correspondent

Private James Brown serving in France during the World War I was amazed and delighted when he had a surprise visitor all the way from England.

Prince, an Irish terrier, was so upset when Private Brown was posted overseas that he decided to go and find him. He left the family home in London and befriended some other soldiers who were heading across the Channel to France. Prince used his tracking skills and what must have been a sixth sense to find his beloved master holed up in a trench in northern France.

At first, Private Brown's commanding officer did not believe the story, but Prince became the hero of the regiment and fought beside Private Brown for the rest of the war.

PARA DOG WINS A MEDAL

by our history correspondent

The Dickin Medal for animal bravery was awarded to an amazing parachuting dog serving with the SAS in World War II.

Rob, a black and white mongrel, was known as 'para dog' by his fellow SAS comrades. He made over twenty parachute jumps, taking part in landings in North Africa and Italy. He is said to have loved parachuting, jumping out of the plane without a moment's hesitation. When he landed, he lay perfectly still until the parachute was detatched by his handler.

Rob was awarded the Dickin Medal after a mission behind enemy lines, which lasted for a number of months. Rob protected his unit throughout the mission, even when faced with extreme danger. A local aristocrat awarded Rob the medal and Rob thanked him with a shake of his paw.

From the archives

THE STORY OF GREYFRIARS BOBBY

by our history correspondent

In 1858, a man named John Gray was buried in Greyfriars Churchyard. For 14 years his devoted dog kept a careful watch over his grave in what is probably the most amazing display of dog devotion in history.

After John Gray's funeral, his faithful dog, Bobby, settled on his grave, his head in his paws and refused to move. The law at the time didn't allow dogs in graveyards, and so Bobby was driven out. But every day he came back to lie sadly by his master's grave. In the end, the law was changed and Bobby was allowed to stay. It didn't matter what the weather was like, Bobby refused to move from his dead master's side. After Bobby's own death, 14 years later, a statue was built to remember the faithful dog who really proved that there is no love like a dog's love.

Chapter Eight

Wow oh wow! This invite has gone up on the fridge – I am SO excited! I love parties! Wag. Wag.

I hope there's cake. **Yum!** And sausage rolls! **Double yum!** And pizza! **Yowzer!** I CAN'T wait!! My tummy is growling at the thought.

> Please come to Poppy's Party.
>
> Come to our house and meet our newest family member!
> On Saturday at 2pm.
>
> Love
>
> Molly (and her mum and dad)

Molly's really excited too. She has asked her mum to write down all the things she needs to do before the party. Here's the list . . .

Before the Party

1. Write your guest list.

2. Make some cute invitations and pass them out to your friends. Make them look as pretty as possible. Don't forget the time, date and place where the party is being held.

On The Day Of The Party

Garden

1. Check that the gate is closed and there are no holes in the fence.

2. Have shovels or bags on hand to pick up any messes when they happen!

3. Put mum's delicate flowerpots in the garage.

4. Have enough balls and dog toys available for Poppy so she doesn't start playing with your friends' toys.

During the party

1. If any presents are opened, throw away all wrapping paper, ribbons and bows straight away where Poppy can't reach them and eat them. She could hurt herself.

2. Think of some fun doggie games like relay races, hide and seek, and hide the treats.

3. Get disposable cameras and give them to your friends so they can have souvenirs of all the fun!

Wow oh wow oh wow! I am SO excited! Jump in mud roll around shake my fur excited.

Thump tail thump!

Ooh, ooh look! People are arriving! **Ooh, ooh,** they've got presents. And they're all for ME! **Wowzer!**

Ooh, ooh, dog snacks! **Yummy! Slurp.**

Ooh, a new collar. It's pink and shiny. I love it!

Wow oh wow oh wow! Dog treats.

Mmmmm. Slurp.

And a new rubber bone. Wow! AND a new rubber ball. Chase. Chase. Pant. Ooh, more dog treats. Yum, yum, bum scrum.

Oh.

Molly's mum has taken them away. She thinks I've had too many. I am sad now.
Hide head in paws sad. Sniff. But Molly picks me up and cuddles me. She whispers to me not to worry, there will be lots of treats all afternoon. Molly wants us to play games. Wow oh wow! I am happy again! I love games.
We play hunt the treasure. Molly's mum and dad have hidden treats in the garden and we have to find them. And the best bit is whatever we find we can EAT! Wow oh wow!

I find doggie choc drops. Slurp. Boiled sweets. Crunch. Mini sausages. Gobble.

I feel a bit sick now.

Just as well Molly's mum is putting everyone into teams to play relay games. This is **FUN!** **Run, run. Pant. Pant.** We win! We all get a prize. The girls get bracelets. BORING! I get a sausage. YUM! I **LOVE** parties!

I am tired now. I feel very sleepy. I close my eyes and put my head in my paws. I am starting to dream about eating the biggest bone in the world when I am woken by everyone ooh-ing and ahh-ing. I sit up and **WOW OH WOW OH WOW!**

Molly's mum and dad are carrying the **HUGEST** cake I have ever seen. It's almost as big as **Bernie** and that is BIG!

And guess what? It is made of dog food and decorated with the most bacon and sausages I have ever seen. **Wowzer!**

Poppy's Cake Recipe

What you need:

- 3 tins of dog food
- Bacon
- Sausages
- Dog treats
- Large bowl
- Large plate

What to do:

Empty the three tins of dog food into the bowl. Place it in the fridge overnight to set. Cook the sausages and bacon and leave overnight to cool. The next day, take the bowl of dog food out of the fridge, place the plate on top of the bowl and, turning it over carefully, empty out the contents. It should have set into the bowl's shape. Now take the sausages and place them right around the sides of the cake. Take the bacon and arrange it on the top of the cake. Finally take the dog treats and use them to spell out your dog's name. And – hey presto! – a cake fit for your best canine friend.

Triple yum. Slurp. Slurp. Slurp.

Delicious! Molly takes lots of photos of me eating a piece of cake. She says I look cute especially as I now have dog food all round my mouth. **Hee hee**. She is ***FUNNY***.

All too soon, the party is over and all Molly's friends start to leave, with doggie bags for all their pets. **Pat. Pat. Stroke. Stroke.**

Parties are **brilliant**.

Oh no. Just had a thought. The party has reminded me that it's **Bernie's** birthday next week.

What shall I do?
What shall I give him?
Something nice to cheer him up.
He'll be all on his own. If only people saw how wonderful he is, rather than how **big** he is.

I feel sad. I miss **Bernie**. Sigh. I wonder whether Tallulah has received my letter. I'm sure she'll come up trumps.

Oh I know! I know! A poem! Wag. Wag. Then he'll know how much he means to me!

Right, let me think. **Um, er, um.** Hang on. **Um. Um.** No. It's no good, I can't think of anything. Sigh. It's not fair! I'm never going to be able to write anything!

I've got it! **Woof! Woof! Alfie!** Wag. Wag. He's super-intelligent. Even more clever than Molly and she got a gold star from school just the other day. Wag. Wag.

As soon as Molly's mum starts the housework I shall sneak off. Wag. Wag. It's not very far. I'll be back before anyone notices I've even gone. **Hurray!**

Later...

Alfie meets me at the door.

He leads me straight into Professor Pemberton's library. **Wow oh wow,** what an amazing room. There are books from ceiling

to floor. Rows and rows of books. Professor Pemberton must be super-amazingly clever. **Wag. Wag.**

'So **Poppy**,' says **Alfie,** 'what can I do for you?'

I explain about **Bernie's** birthday and that I want to write a poem, but don't know how.

Alfie smiles at me reassuringly. 'My dear **Poppy**,' he says. 'Nothing could be simpler.'

Wow oh wow! I hope so!

Alfie writes down a few rules first.

Alfie's guide to writing a poem

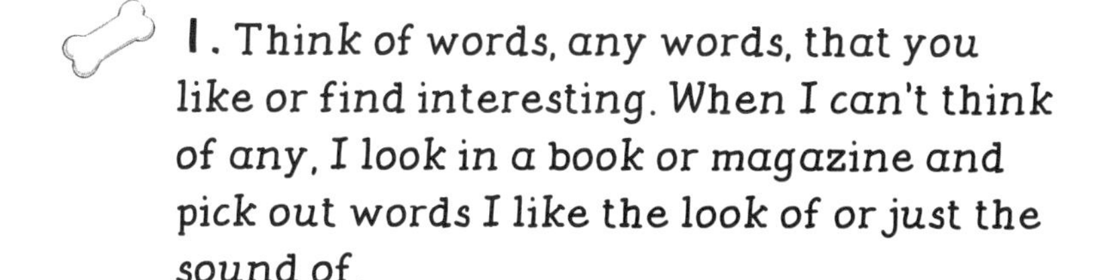

1. Think of words, any words, that you like or find interesting. When I can't think of any, I look in a book or magazine and pick out words I like the look of or just the sound of.

2. When you've written down ten or twenty shuffle them round in any order you like and divide them up into several groups until you get an image, a sound or an idea that interests you.

3. Take out any words that you don't want and fit in new words including words like 'the', 'but' and 'then'.

4. Once you've got that far, it's not too hard to arrange these words to make up a verse or a rhyme or a freestyle non-rhyming poem.

Then we both have a go at writing poems. Alfie says I am a natural. I think I am a really good poet too! **Wag. Wag.**

Here they are! **Look! Look!**

Bones

Bones are great. They taste yummy.
They're just the right size for my tummy.
They can be chewed or licked.
Gnawed, gulped or picked.
If there were no bones it wouldn't be funny.

Here's one Alfie wrote about me!
I think it's **NICE.**

Poppy

Crazy

Understanding

Dumb

Eats. A lot.

Licks

Everyone

Silly

WOW oh wow! Cool huh? Here's the poem I wrote for **Bernie**. It is very good. Even if I say so myself! **Wag. Wag.**

My friend Bernie

Pretty

Awesome

Enormous

Nice

Not naughty

Great big paws

And that's my best friend, Bernie

I run all the way home from Alfie's. Fast as I can. Run. Run. **Pant. Pant.**

I want to tell Charlie my poem. He pretends that he thinks poems and flowers and stuff are girlie and stupid. But I caught him watching 'Lady And The Tramp' with a tear in his eye. He said it was hayfever. But I know different. **Wag. Wag.**

Charlie is a big old **SOFTIE** at heart. **Wag. Wag.**

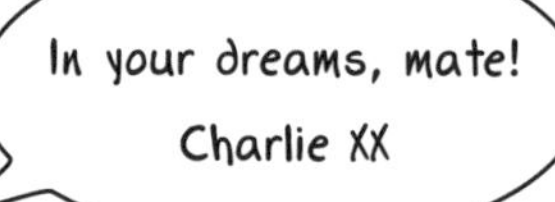

When I get home, I can hear everyone in the kitchen. I trot straight in. A letter has arrived about a fund-raising reunion for all the old dogs from the London Dogs' Home.

The Home needs to make money. Very very fast. It's an **ENORMOUS** amount of money. So much I can't even imagine it. I tried to picture it in bones. But even then I couldn't do it. **Sigh.**

Otherwise it might have to close.

I am very sad. And worried. What will happen

to Bernie and all the other dogs then? Oh why, oh why can't some family as nice as Molly's family adopt **Bernie**? **Sigh**.

Molly's dad has told me not to worry. He's said it will all be fine. I wish I could believe him. **Sigh**.

Chapter Nine

by Poppy

We head into the grounds of the London Dogs' Home. As soon as Molly lets me off my lead, I run helter-skelter towards the other dogs.

I am SO excited!

Hi! Hi, friends! Hi, everyone! Bernie cuffs me fondly with his huge paw. **Alfie** wags his tail happily.

Just then an excited yapping fills my ears. I turn round as a familiar figure prances delicately towards me.

TALLULAH!!

Oh wow! I am such a HAPPY dog! We run. We play. We run again. We chase our tails in excitement. I can't believe she's here. She's really here. She smells GOOD!

'Darling, you look wonderful!' she smiles. 'And don't worry, I brought the little pressie you asked for. It's absolutely super, **Bernie** will love it. You're an absolute sweetie to think of it. And I have a feeling everything is going to turn out just fine.'

Tallulah is here with Kerry. They got the letter about the fund-raising too.

Oooh. Oooh. And **MaViS** is here. She winks at me from Stella the Fortune Teller's side.

I am one happy pup. I **LOVE** my friends. This is better than a peanut sandwich with onion gravy and birthday cake on top!
Woof. Woof.

We run around the grounds happily. It is fun. There is so much to see! There are loads and loads of stalls.

Even better there's lots and lots to eat!

Hot dogs. Yum!

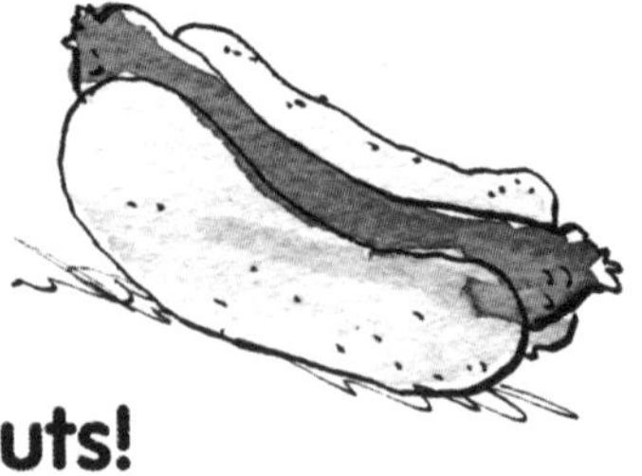

Doughnuts! Scrum!

Cakes. Slurp, slurp, slurp!

Eventually we all land in an exhausted full-tummy heap on the ground. **Bernie** is still convinced he has fleas and is busy scratching behind his ears.

Tallulah watches him for a while. Then she says, 'Why does a dog scratch himself?'

'I don't know,' yawns **Alfie**. 'Why does a dog scratch himself?'

'Because no one else knows where he itches.' Tallulah giggles.

Hee, hee! She's funny. We all roll around on the floor laughing. **Woof. Woof.**

'Actually, seeing you, Tallulah, has reminded

me of another old joke,' says **Alfie**. 'What kind of dog likes baths?

'I know! I know!' I shout. 'A shampoodle! '

Thump. Thump.

Molly's dad's mobile phone rings. **Loudly.** We all stop laughing and remember why we are here. For a minute we all look at each other sadly. Tallulah winks at us. 'What do you get when you cross a dog and a phone?'

'I don't know,' I say.

'A golden receiver, of course,' she grins.

I think my tail might fall off as I am laughing so much. **Hee hee hee! Woof woof!**

Mavis trots over to see what all the commotion is about. Not one to be outdone, she joins in.

'How do you catch a runaway dog?' she asks.

'No idea.' I groan. I am lying on my tummy. It hurts. I have laughed too much. **Ow!**

'Well, hide behind a tree and make a noise like a bone, of course,' she smirks.

Hee. Hee. Hee. I roll over and accidentally bump into **Bernie.** He nudges me playfully out of the way with his nose. I love **Bernie.**

'Come on **Bernie,** you must know a joke,' I say. He smiles sadly. 'I only know one,' he sighs. 'I dare say you'll have heard it before.'

'Come on, ducks,' says **MaViS**. 'Spit it out.'

Bernie sighs loudly. 'OK, but don't blame me, if it's not funny. How do you stop a dog from smelling?'

'Don't know,' we chorus.

'Put a peg on its nose.'

Hee! Hee! Hee! I really think my sides might split. I never knew there were so many funny dog jokes!

Tap. Tap. Tap. The lady in charge of the Home is standing on a stage. All the other staff are standing behind her.

I remember why we are here. I feel sick.

The lady starts talking.

'Ladies and gentlemen, thank you so much for coming to support us today. I cannot tell you how much we appreciate your efforts on behalf of the London Dogs' Home. With your help we have managed to raise a thousand pounds.'

Everyone starts clapping and cheering.
Clap. Clap, Clap.

Me, Bernie, MaViS, ALfie and Tallulah all wag our tails as hard as we can.

Wag. Wag.
Thump. Thump. Thump.

The lady holds her hands up in the air.

'Sadly, that amount alone is not enough to keep the Home open.'

Bernie hides his head in his paws.

The lady holds her hands up again. 'But fortunately we don't have to worry about

that, thanks to one very generous dog owner. Kerry Merringue, who I'm sure you'll all recognise as an ex-member of the girl group Just Girls and now a huge Hollywood star. Kerry has kindly donated one million pounds!'

Wowzer! Kerry bounds on to the stage dressed in a bright pink catsuit. **Woof Woof.**

Boy oh boy. Tallulah does a somersault in the air. **Bernie's** huge tail leaves a small crater in the ground he's wagging it so hard.

I chase my tail, round and round and round. Now I am DIZZY!

MaVis trots over, 'All right, treacle,' she says, nodding in the direction of the stage. 'I told yer, pink would be lucky for yer, didn't I? Now all you need is that big house. And somefink tells me that is on its way.'

A huge pink lorry pulls up outside the home. Tallulah smiles. 'That's your gift.'

A man climbs out of the front seat and walks round to the back of the lorry. He seems to be

struggling to pull something out. **Hee hee hee**, he looks funny.

A minute later, he's struggling under the weight of the biggest doghouse you have ever seen. **Wow oh wow**. It is as big as the shed. I don't reckon even the Queen's corgis have a kennel that big. **Wow oh wow!** Tallulah and I grin at each other. Even I didn't expect it to be this fantastic!

There is a big pink ribbon tied round the middle. Attached to the ribbon is a big label that says...

Everyone at the home rushes towards the doghouse in excitement.

Woof. Woof. Woof.

Kerry is still on the stage. She taps the microphone . . .

'Ladies and gentlemen, when I received the letter from the Home asking for help to keep it open, the least I could do was make a donation, after all if it wasn't for the Home's good work, I wouldn't have my darling Tallulah.

'So when a second letter came, telling me about **Bernie** and the fact it's so hard to find him a home because he's so big, I immediately bought the biggest doghouse I could find. I thought to myself that if I can't provide **Bernie** with a home, I CAN provide him with the best house a dog could want. I hope this will mean that some kind family with a large garden will now be able to adopt **Bernie**. If he brings them just a tenth of the happiness my Tallulah has brought me, they'll be a lucky family indeed.'

Clap. Clap. Clap. Clap.

Everyone is applauding. And cheering.

Boy oh boy are they loud! Bernie is sitting open-mouthed, staring at his enormous doghouse in disbelief. **Wag. Wag.**

Luckily Kerry is too busy, smiling, waving and signing autographs to take any notice of the lady from the Home who is frantically trying to tell her that she doesn't know anything about the second letter.

Woof. Woof.

Of course she doesn't. It was from me! **Hee. Hee.** I faked it and asked Tallulah to find a way of getting Kerry to read it, so she would buy **Bernie** a big house to sleep in. Tallulah is so CLEVER. **Wag. Wag.** I knew she'd do it! And the rest, as they say is history. Boy oh boy, I've always wanted to say that.

Hee. Hee.

Later...

Alfie and **Mavis** have gone. Tallulah is leaving in a bright, pink, stretch limousine with Kerry. Everyone is staring and staring. What a way to go! **Wag. Wag.**

Molly comes over to collect me. I am sad. Even though **Bernie** now has a nice new doghouse to sleep in, I don't want to leave him at the Home. He licks my nose sadly. **Lick. Lick.** Sniff.

He slowly starts to walk away. I feel like crying. I am so sad.

But Molly's grinning. She calls **Bernie** back. She bends down and ruffles his fur. 'Where are you going, **Bernie?** You've got a nice new home to go to, with a great new family and their little puppy.'

Wow oh wow oh wow! Where, Molly? Where? I hope it's near me. I am so excited. **Wag Wag.**

But it gets better . . .

'Yes, **Bernie**, you're coming home with us.' says Molly's dad. 'We'd already decided that if the Home had to close, we were going to take you. Even if it was going to be a squash. But now you've got a great big comfortable house of your own to live in, that's even better! We've got a great big garden for it to go in. Welcome to the family **Bernie**!'

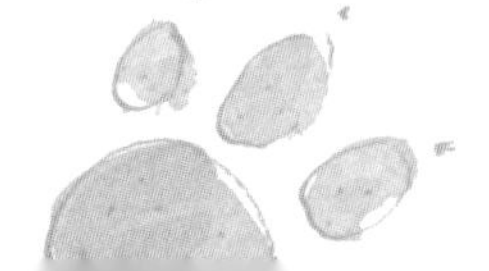

Molly leans down and hugs him.

THIS IS BETTER THAN WALKIES!

Woof.
Woof.

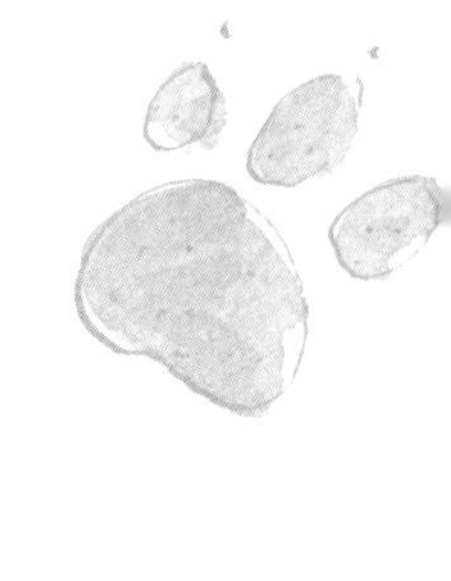

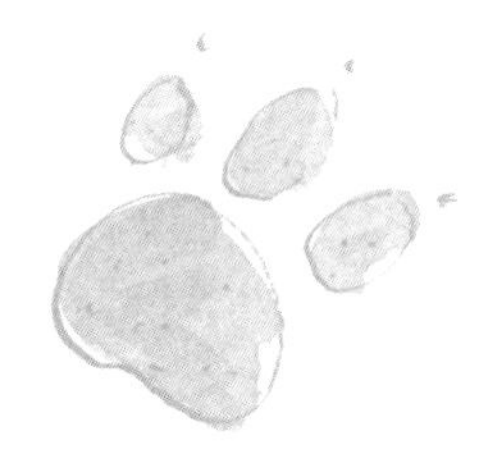

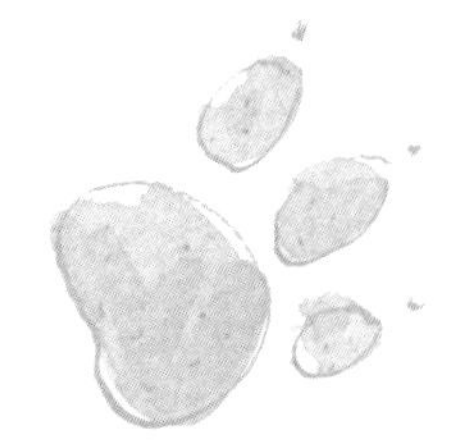

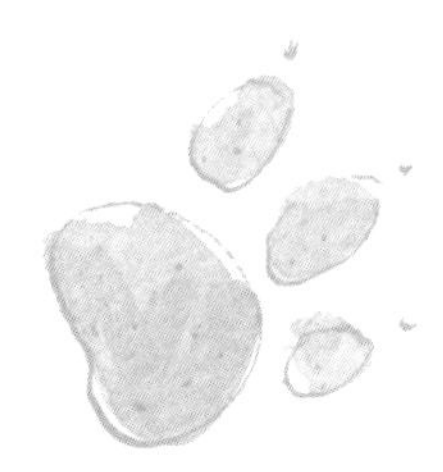

by Poppy

Me, **Bernie**, Molly, Nathan, and Molly's mum and dad are all out on walkies. It's **SO** great.

When we get to the park, Molly lets **Bernie** and me off our leads. **Bernie's** so excited to be out in the real world. We run. We jump and roll over and over until we land in an exhausted heap. **Pant. Pant.**

Now all my favourite people are under one roof and Bernie's part of the family. Things just couldn't be any better.

Not even if you threw in a lifetime's supply of Doggie Treats. **Wag. Wag.**

The End

Woof!

YOUR VERY OWN PUP'S LIFE

Hi, hi there. **Me** again. I hope you liked my book. To **thank you** for reading it, I've included this bit at the back – it's for you to fill in things about your dog, or the dog you really really wish you had.
Gotta run. I've got a ball to catch!

My dog's name is/ would be . . .

....

....

His or her breed is/ would be . . .

....

....

I chose this dog because . . .

....

....

....

My dog is/ would be special because . . .

....

....

....

My dog's favourite thing is/ would be . . .

....

....

....

....

If I could buy anything in Tallulah's catalogue, it would be . . .

....

....

....

The thing my dog would most like me to make for him/ her is . . .

....

....

....

The thing he/ she would like the least is . . .

....

....

....

My favourite dog joke is ...

Here is my dog poem ...

My favourite dog story is . . .

....

....

....

....

....

....

....

....

....

....

....

....

Here's another fantastic dog recipe . . .

....

....

....

....

Other amazing dog facts . . .

....

....

....

Great party games for pups . . .

....

....

....

....

My favourite dog film is . . .

....

....

....

....

....

....

I give it 🐾 🐾 🐾 🐾 out of four paw prints

Signed: ....

Would you like to help dogs like Poppy and Bernie?

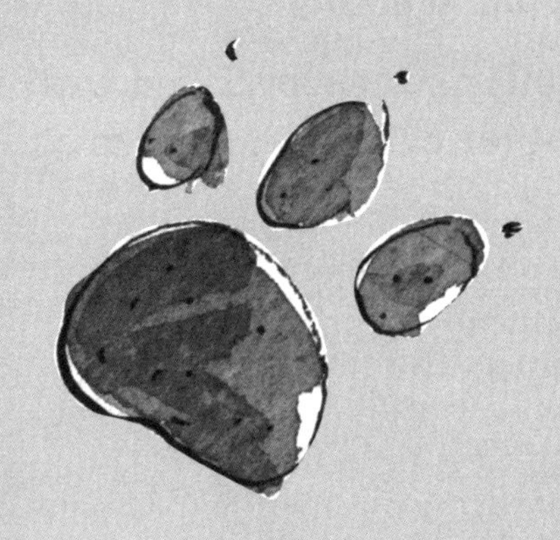

Here's where to start ...

Contact the National Canine Defence League www.ncdl.org.uk and find out how you can:

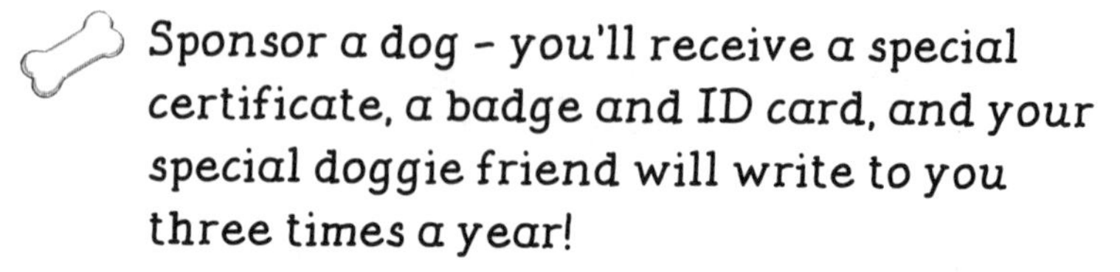
Sponsor a dog - you'll receive a special certificate, a badge and ID card, and your special doggie friend will write to you three times a year!

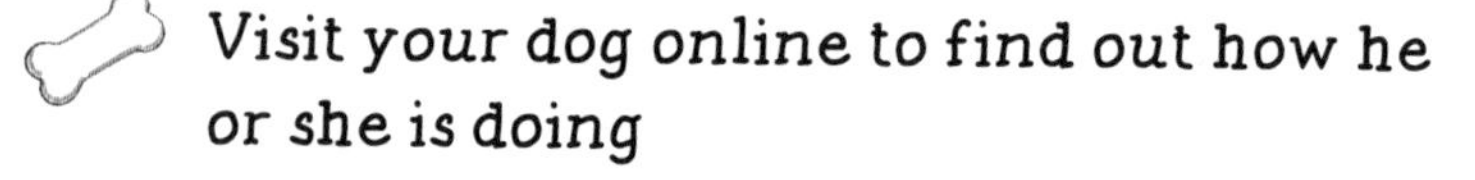
Visit your dog online to find out how he or she is doing

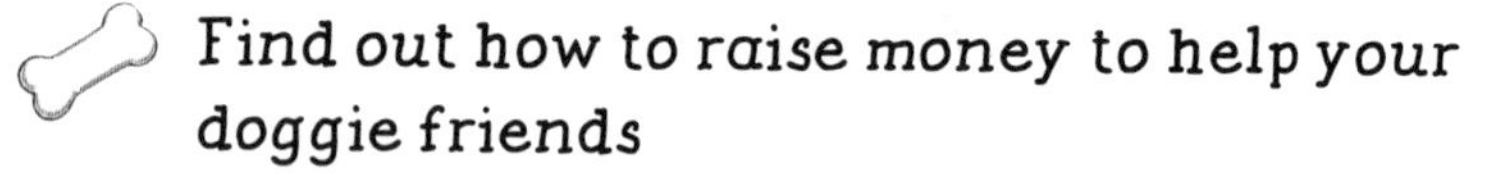
Find out how to raise money to help your doggie friends

Contact the RSPCA www.rspca.org.uk to:

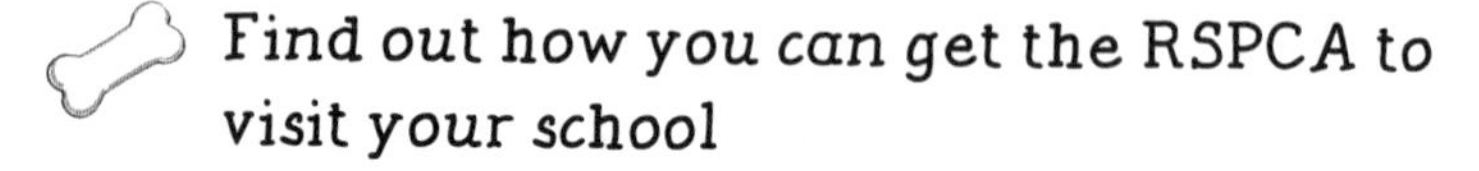
Find out how you can get the RSPCA to visit your school

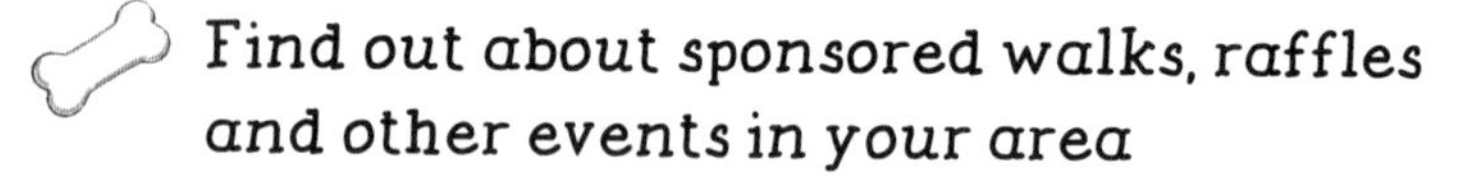
Find out about sponsored walks, raffles and other events in your area

For your local animal shelter try www.rescuepet.org.uk or look in your Yellow Pages telephone directory.

Alternatively, why don't you try one of these ingenious ideas to raise money for your local dogs' home?

- Organise a sponsored dog walk
- Bake and sell bone-shaped cakes to your friends and family
- Hold a sponsored doggie-talk with your friends - see if you can speak in only barks and growls for a whole day!